PICTURE POOKS

I'M A PIG

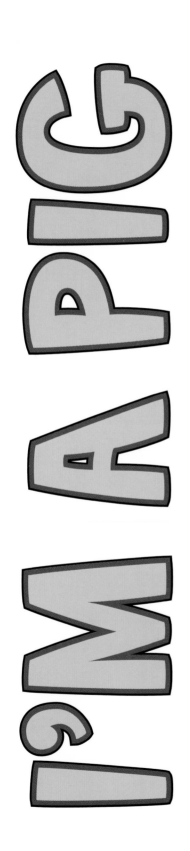

By Sarah Weeks ♥ Illustrated by Holly Berry

LAURA GERINGER BOOKS
An Imprint of HarperCollinsPublishers

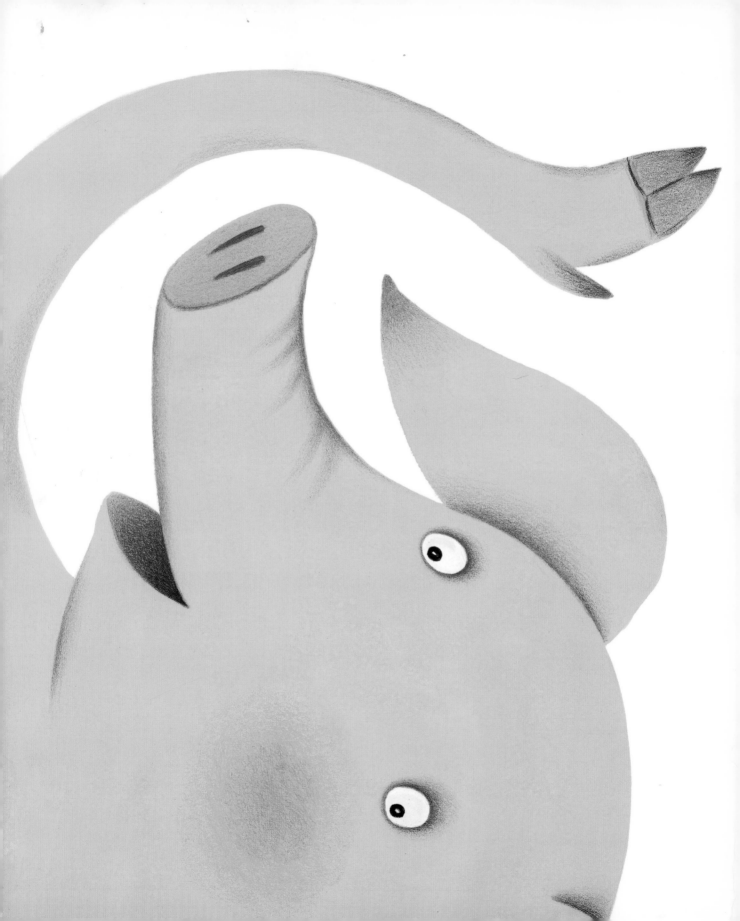

I'm a pig, I'm a pig,

and I don't give a fig
if you call me a pig,
'cause that's what I am.
I'm a pig, I'm a pig,

and I'm happy as a clam

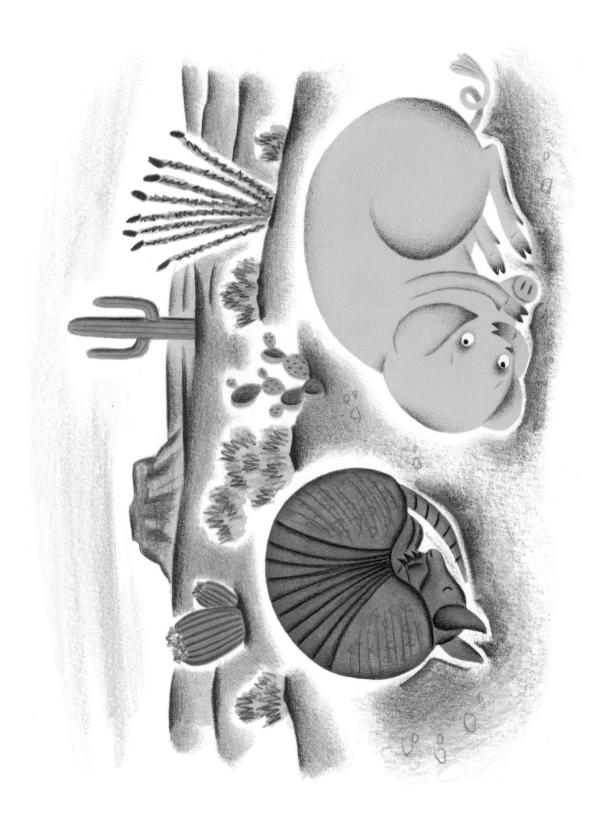

that I'm not an armadillo

or a lion

or a lamb.

I'm a pig, I'm a pig,
and I'll do a happy jig
if you say, "What a pig!"

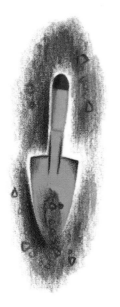

For there isn't any doubt—
I'm a pig, I'm a pig, I'm a pig
from my tail to my snout,
and acting like a pig
is what it's all about.

I can oink at the moon,

I can wallow in the mud,

I can grin like a goon
as I gobble down a spud.
And I think to be pink
is an honor and a treat.
Besides, it goes so nicely
with my shiny black feet.

I'm a pig, I'm a pig,
and my brain is very big.
Nothing's smarter than a pig.
Look it up—it's true!

I'm a pig, I'm a pig.
I don't blame you if you're blue.
If I were only human,
I'd be disappointed too.

I can just lie around
grunting grunts all day
with my nose to the ground—
not a truffle gets away.

And I feel I could squeal—I'm so happy to be me!
A pig is just the absolutely perfect thing to be.
I'm a pig, I'm a pig,
and I don't give a fig
if you call me a pig,
'cause that's what I am.

I'm a pig, I'm a pig,
and I'm happy as a clam
that I'm not a little puppy
or a guppy or a camel

or a goose

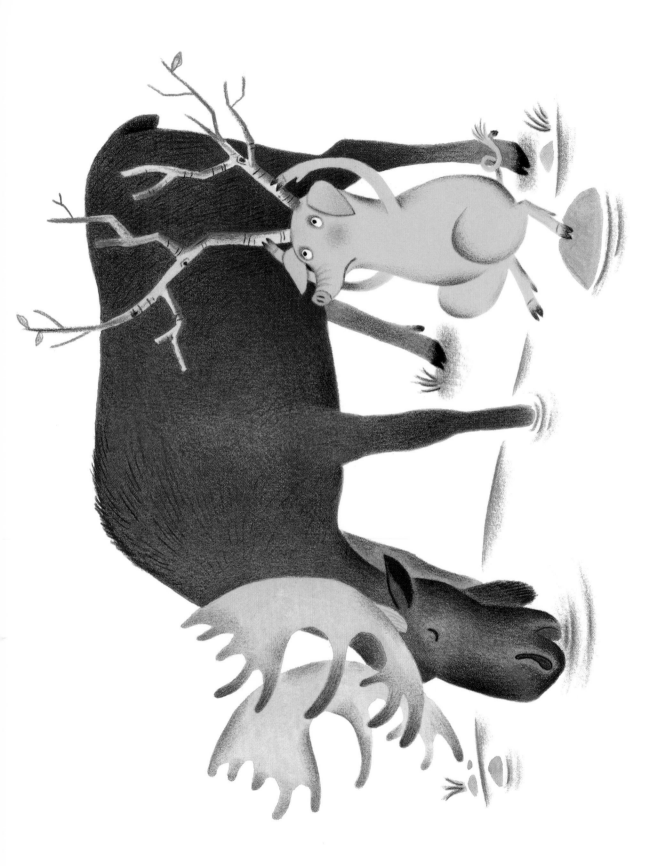

or a moose

or a yellow-bellied mammal—no,
I'm not an armadillo or a lion or a lamb.
I am simply tickled pink

to be exactly what I am.

To Gabe and Natty
—S.W.

To Ellie—
May you always be happy to be just who you are
—H.B.

Library of Congress Cataloging-in-Publication Data
Weeks, Sarah.   I'm a pig / by Sarah Weeks ; illustrated by Holly Berry.— 1st ed.   p. cm.   Summary: In rhyming text, a happy pig proclaims the joys of her porcine life.
ISBN 0-694-01075-8 — ISBN 0-06-074344-1 (lib. bdg.)   [1. Identity—Fiction. 2. Self-esteem—Fiction. 3. Pigs—Fiction.]
I. Berry, Holly, ill.   II. Title.   PZ8.3.W4125Im 2005   [E]—dc22   2004002898   CIP   AC   Typography by Alicia Mikles   1 2 3 4 5 6 7 8 9 10   ❖   First Edition